Sleep Well, Sweet Dreams
The Tale of the
TOOTH FAIRY

by
Ian Wilms

Illustrations by Mike Motz

Copyright Registration 1085530 - March 25, 2011

CANADA

By Ian Patrick Wilms

ISBN 978-0-9876753-0-9

This book was a family affair.

To my loving wife, Kim. Thank you for supporting and believing in my dreams.

Inspired by my wonderful children. Thank you for all of your creative input.

Edited by my creative and gifted mother, Oonagh.

Special thanks to my nieces, Menaka and Meghan, and good friend, Bonnie.

In memory of, and dedicated to my incredible Father, Heiner.

An inspiration to us all.

Sleep well, sweet dreams is what he said to my brother and I

every night as he tucked us into our beds.

It was bed time.
Alexandra, Nicholas, and Jack were bundled
under the covers of their parent's bed,
waiting patiently for Mom
to read them their bedtime story.

Nicholas, who had just lost his tooth,
said, "Mom, do I have to give
my tooth to the Tooth Fairy tonight?
I want to keep it." It was then
that Mom felt it was time for the children to
learn the tale of the Tooth Fairy.

In a wonderful land, far away, there is a
beautiful place called the Pearly White City,
where the Tooth Fairy lives and watches over
the people of this friendly City.

It is here that the people of
the Pearly White City
make the big teeth to replace
the baby teeth that we lose
as we are growing up.

Every night the magical Tooth Fairy
flies around the world, collecting baby
teeth that have been kindly donated
and put under pillows by the children.

The Tooth Fairy then brings these baby teeth back to the tooth making factory in the Pearly White City. She mixes the baby teeth with water, apples, and special fairy potion to create the big teeth that start to grow in our mouths. She delivers these teeth to the children while they are sleeping.

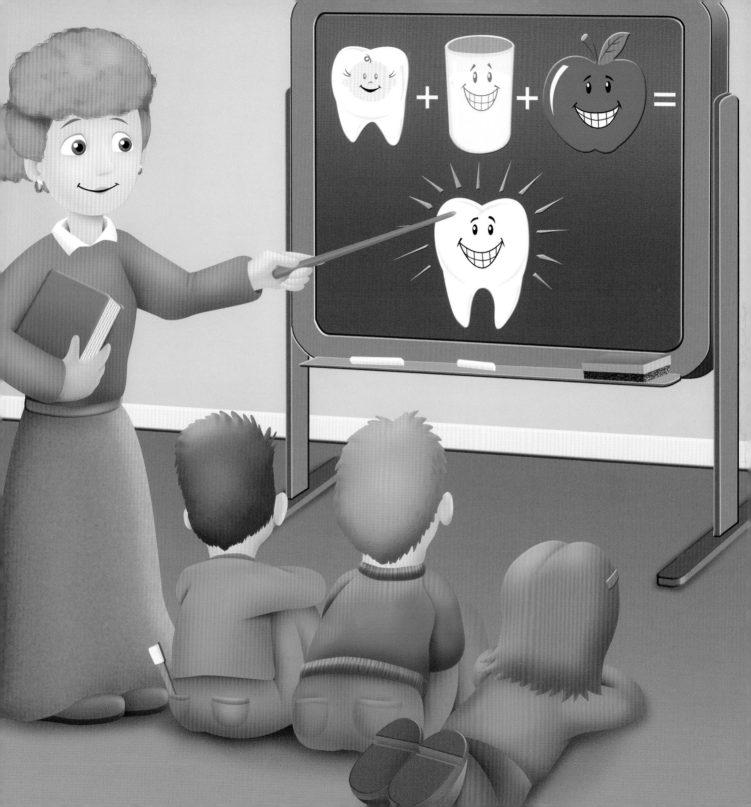

Unfortunately, all is not perfect in this beautiful land. There is one person that does not like the Tooth Fairy bringing nice, new teeth to the children. That person is the terrible Prince Plaque, Lord of Cavity Castle. The nasty Prince wants children to get cavities because he knows that the Tooth Fairy cannot use teeth with cavities in her big teeth potion.

Prince Plaque's evil wizards are always creating new sugar potions to weaken the teeth walls of the Pearly White City and to create cavities in children's teeth. If Prince Plaque can break down the teeth walls and destroy the tooth making factory, then he alone will become the ruler of the Pearly White City and beautiful, white teeth will be gone forever!

For as long as we can remember,
Prince Plaque and his army of Tartar
Troopers have attacked the teeth walls of the
Pearly White City in an effort to enter the city
and destroy the tooth making factory.

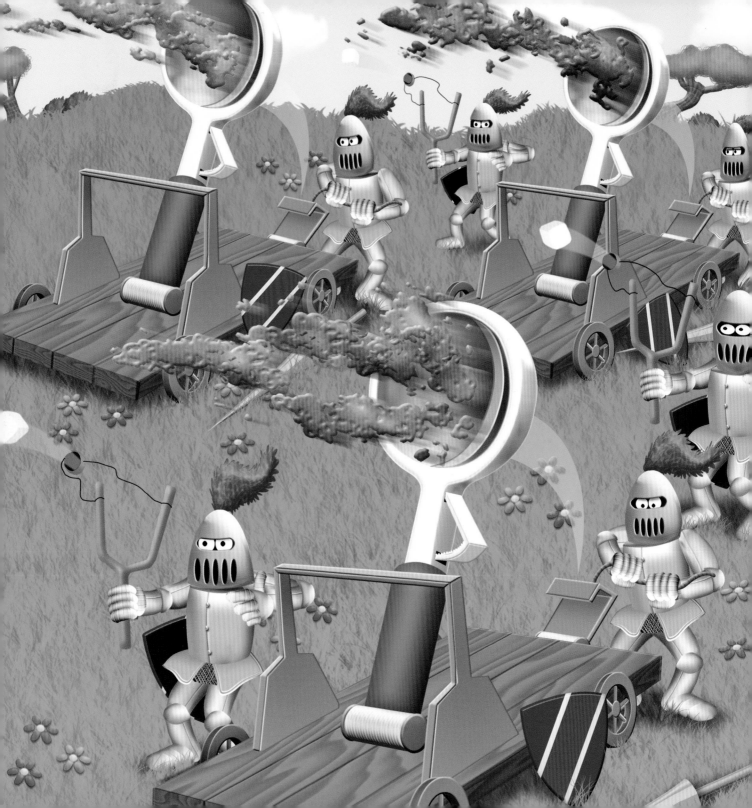

Three times a day, and especially around the time we eat breakfast, lunch, and dinner, Prince Plaque will attack. His forces use Sugar Slings and Cavity Catapults to fling ooze and guck at the beautiful teeth walls of the Pearly White City.

Fortunately, the Pearly White City is
protected by Sir Brushalot and his Knights of
Floss. Every time Prince Plaque attacks,
Sir Brushalot, riding his famous horse,
DEN-TIST, charges out of the city and
chases the evil troopers away.

The attack by the Tartar Troopers
is over quickly, but the damage
they do to the teeth walls remains and
looks horrible. If the guck and slime is not
removed speedily, the harm it does to the teeth
walls can become much worse.

The Knights of Floss quickly get
to work. They fix the damage that
occurred during the battle and
polish the walls of the Pearly White City
back to their magnificent brightness.

The Tooth Fairy and the people
of the Pearly White City are forever
grateful for the bravery of
Sir Brushalot and his Knights of Floss.

Once again, Prince Plaque has been
beaten back, but he will never give up.
We must make sure we do everything we
can to help the Tooth Fairy and Sir Brushalot
defeat the forces of Prince Plaque.

Mom looked around
and realized the bed was
now empty and the children
were gone.

She found Alexandra, Nicholas, and
Jack in the bathroom, brushing
and flossing their teeth.
"We've got to fight Prince Plaque
Mommy!" they all yelled together.

Sleep well,
Sweet dreams!

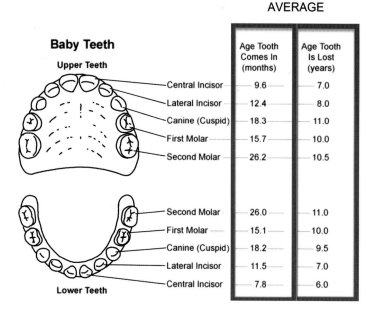

Baby Teeth

Upper Teeth

| | AVERAGE | |
Baby Teeth	Age Tooth Comes In (months)	Age Tooth Is Lost (years)
Central Incisor	9.6	7.0
Lateral Incisor	12.4	8.0
Canine (Cuspid)	18.3	11.0
First Molar	15.7	10.0
Second Molar	26.2	10.5
Second Molar	26.0	11.0
First Molar	15.1	10.0
Canine (Cuspid)	18.2	9.5
Lateral Incisor	11.5	7.0
Central Incisor	7.8	6.0

Lower Teeth

For more important information about your teeth, please visit our website.

www.brushalot.com

PLUS, free coloring pages to download!

**** IMPORTANT ****
**** only water at bedtime, no juice please ****

Dates teeth first appeared

1st _____

2nd _____

3rd _____

4th _____

5th _____

Dates teeth first lost

1st _____

2nd _____

3rd _____

4th _____

5th _____